Henry Solly

Our English Presbyterian Forefathers

SALZWASSER VERLAG

Henry Solly

Our English Presbyterian Forefathers

Reprint of the original, first published in 1859.

1st Edition 2022 | ISBN: 978-3-37513-330-6

Verlag (Publisher): Salzwasser Verlag GmbH, Zeilweg 44, 60439 Frankfurt, Deutschland
Vertretungsberechtigt (Authorized to represent): E. Roepke, Zeilweg 44, 60439 Frankfurt, Deutschland
Druck (Print): Books on Demand GmbH, In de Tarpen 42, 22848 Norderstedt, Deutschland

OUR

ENGLISH PRESBYTERIAN

FOREFATHERS;

A SKETCH OF THEIR HISTORY AND PRINCIPLES, FROM
THE TIME OF THE REFORMATION
TO THE PRESENT DAY.

BY HENRY SOLLY,

MINISTER OF THE ENGLISH PRESBYTERIAN CHAPEL, LANCASTER.

London:
E. WHITFIELD, STRAND. LANCASTER: RICHARDSON.
1859.
Price Sixpence.

PREFACE.

An eminent Independent Minister* observed a few years ago to the writer, in reply to a remark by the latter connecting modern Unitarians with Presbyterians, — " Presbyterians I understand, and Unitarians I understand, but Presbyterian Unitarians, or Unitarian Presbyterians, I cannot understand at all." A similar ignorance respecting the later history of the men who once played so mighty a part in English history, and concerning the derivation of the sect now called Unitarians, will be found pervading all classes, even the best informed on other topics. Nay, many of the actual descendants of the noble-hearted men who bore witness to what they believed to be God's truth through cruel persecution, with unfaltering constancy, know little or nothing of the history of their ancestors, and of the Christian society in which their fathers worshipped. Hundreds of young people are growing up without ever having heard of names and deeds which should stir their youthful hearts with enthusiasm, and speak to their consciences in thrilling tones of the solemn call to honour, in like manner, their Saviour and their God. But the history of such a body as that of the English Presbyterians, especially of the inner life and principle that animated them, the results that have ensued, the meaning and responsibilities of the position bequeathed to their descen-

* The Rev. Newman Hall, B.A.

dants, are not matters that can be neglected by those descendants without dishonour and immeasurable loss. The causes that have led to this strange indifference and ignorance are glanced at in the letters to be found at the end of the following sketch ;* but the whole subject deserves patient and thorough investigation, by a careful perusal of the chief works illustrating it, especially Neal's "History of the Puritans," and J. J. Tayler's admirable "Retrospect of the Religious Life of England." And my present endeavour having been not to satisfy, but to awaken, the desire for information on the subject, and guide it to the sources where fuller supplies may be obtained, I have done little more than present a very condensed statement of the facts and views recorded by those writers. Many of the other works which should be consulted will be found referred to in the following pages, but there are various valuable biographies and local histories which might be read with interest and profit, that I have not yet had time or opportunity to examine.

* See Appendix.

OUR

ENGLISH PRESBYTERIAN
FOREFATHERS.

English Presbyterianism took its rise, in actual outward form, in the days of Queen Elizabeth, and was the first, as well as the most powerful development of Puritan resistance to the Romanist tendencies of that monarch. The great historian of the Puritans * observes, "Her Majesty was afraid of reforming too far; she was desirous to retain images in churches, crucifixes and crosses, vocal and instrumental music with all the popish garments; it is not therefore to be wondered that in reviewing the liturgy of King Edward, no alterations were made in favour of those who now began to be called Puritans, from their attempting a purer form of worship and discipline than had yet been established." And what was far more serious even then, was her Majesty's determination on the one hand to retain the spiritual despotism of the Pope in her own hands, and to enforce, on the other, an absolute uniformity of doctrine and discipline among all classes of her subjects. The Act for the Supremacy of the Crown in matters ecclesiastical and spiritual, and the Act for Uniformity in the Prayer and Service of the Church were both passed in the session of 1558-9, and, as Neal remarks, "Sad were the consequences of these two laws both to the Papists and Puritans." Out of the former Act grew the iniquitous Court of High Commission, which was "the source of the most arbitrary proceedings, and of the most shameful tyranny" in this and the two succeeding reigns. Bishop Burnet tells us that the supremacy given to the Crown by this Act was *short* of the authority possessed by

* Neal's History of the Puritans, vol. I., chap. 4, page 129.—London 1793.

Henry VIII., and of what Elizabeth claimed, for she several
times stretched her prerogative beyond it. It was, of
course, a grievous offence to the earnest Reformers of that
day, who thought they had separated from the Church of
Rome in order that Christ, not the chief Ruler of England,
might be recognised as the true Head of his own Church.*
And as to the Act of Uniformity, Neal observes, " Upon
this fatal rock of uniformity in things merely indifferent
(in the opinion of the imposers), was the peace of the
Church of England split. . . . . . The rigorous
pressing of this Act was the occasion of all the mischiefs
that befel the Church for above 80 years."† The differences
that arose between the advisers of Elizabeth and the
Puritans, as all historians agree, were not doctrinal. Here
and there in the ranks of the latter were found those who
objected to some portion of the Creeds and articles, and
occasionally we meet with Unitarian martyrs to their
belief in the sole deity of one God the Father, as well as
with other forms of heresy. But these were rare exceptions. ‡
The grand origin of dissent in this country—the solemn
protest against a pseudo-protestantism—was the retention
by the Queen and her advisers of those Romish ceremonies,
sentiments, and superstitions, especially of that spiritual
and ecclesiastical despotism, which the continental protestants had shed their blood to abolish, and which were as
manifestly opposed to the word of God as to the spirit of
Christ. It must never be forgotten that the men who took
a leading part in this protest, and who were at length
driven to separate from the Established Church through the
utter failure of their efforts to obtain redress, were with
scarce an exception persons of exemplary piety and learning,
many of them of high station in that church §, clergymen
of all ranks, and animated with a sincere desire not only
for purity of worship, but for Christian union. As it is
essential for a right understanding of the Puritan move-

* See, among other documents of the time, Cartwright's noble "Ad-
monition to Parliament," lib. ii., p. p. 4, 11, quoted by Neal, vol. i., p. 125.

  † p. p. 130, 131.   ‡ p. 213.

§ Heath, Archbishop of York, made an admirable speech in the
House of Lords against the Act of Uniformity.

ment, and the whole subsequent career of the English Presbyterians, to perceive both the character and position of these early Reformers, and the exact nature of the protest which led to separation, without which understanding we should be in danger either of unjustly condemning their conduct or of ignorantly admiring it, it is necessary a short space be devoted to a further and more detailed statement.

The Puritans objected then, among other matters, to the exaltation of Bishops in dignity and power above their brethren, maintaining that all ministers of Christ should be on an equality in these respects, but they also disapproved of the temporal dignities and secular employments of the episcopal bench. They complained of the exorbitant power and jurisdiction of the bishops and their chancellors in the ecclesiastical courts, of the excessive punishments they there inflicted, and of the power of excommunication and absolution being in the hands of laymen. They objected to the titles and offices of archdeacons, deans, chapters, and so forth, as being unscriptural and trenching upon the privileges of the presbyters. They lamented the absence of a godly discipline, and a promiscuous admission of all sorts of persons to the Lord's table. "The Church being described in her articles as a congregation of faithful persons, they thought it necessary that a power should be lodged somewhere to enquire into the qualifications of such as desired to be of her communion."* They did not dispute the lawfulness of set forms of prayer, but at the same time disapproved of several things in the Liturgy, and especially in the Marriage and Burial services. They disliked the enforced reading of the Apocryphal books, and while they did not condemn the use of the printed homilies, they urged that no man should be ordained who was not able to preach his own sermons, and complained of the many "dumb ministers, pluralists, and non-residents" presented to benefices. They maintained that incumbents should be elected to a benefice by the people, not be presented by a patron.

* Neal, vol. 1, chap. v., p. 210.

They disapproved moreover, of the observance of the Church festivals and holidays, of the cathedral mode of worship, of intoning their prayers, of the antiphone, and of musical instruments, as trumpets and organs, which "were not in use until 1200 years after the death of Christ." They scrupled conformity also to the rubrick in the following matters, viz. : making the sign of the Cross in baptism, churching women, the use of godfathers and godmothers, (strongly condemning, and most righteously, the 29th canon, which says of the christening, "No parent shall be urged to be present, nor be admitted to answer as god-father to his own child "); furthermore, they objected to confirming children as soon as they could say the Lord's prayer and the Catechism, of the laying on of hands by the bishop at confirmation, the injunction to kneel at the com-munion of the Lord's Supper, the bowing at the name of Jesus, the use of the ring in marriage, the allowing licenses for private or secret marriages, the wearing of the surplice and many other ceremonies during the celebration of divine service. And lastly, (but we should say chiefly), they pleaded " the natural right that every man has to judge for himself, and make profession of that religion he apprehends most agreeable to truth, as far as it does not affect the peace and safety of the government he lives under; without being determined by the prejudices of education, the laws of civil magistrate, or the decrees of churches, councils, or synods. This principle," says Neal, with his cautious yet noble simplicity, " would effectually put an end to all im-positions, and unless it be allowed, I am afraid our separa-tion from the church of Rome can hardly be justified. The Bible, says Mr. Chillingworth, and that only, is the religion of Protestants ; and every one by making use of the helps and assistances God has put into his hands, must learn and understand it for himself, as well as he can."* Bishop Warburton objects to this great principle being set down as one of the heads of controversy between the Puritans and the Conformists of that day, and maintains that it was " a truth unknown to either party." Now it is

* Neal, vol. I., ch. V., p. 214.

freely granted that the Puritans as a body were very far from fully receiving it, or admitting its legitimate consequences, as certain melancholy facts in their subsequent history prove. But there is also abundant evidence to justify Neal's assertion, and also to show that the Bible was constantly appealed to as the *supreme* arbiter in all disputes. Even the state Church in the 6th of her 39 articles expressly recognises the necessity of proving every thing from the Word of God, while the Puritans when brought before Bishops or Magistrates, constantly rested their vindication upon the above principle.

When the Puritan Clergymen found all their efforts vain to obtain any redress of their grievances, they at length, but with deepest reluctance, seceded from the State Church, and either gave up their livings, or were deprived of them for refusing to conform to the Rubrick. The worship of God according to their own conscience, however, they did did not give up; and many a lonely wood, or silent hilltop, as well as private houses, witnessed the fervent celebration of Divine Worship by these faithful servants of Christ and their lay supporters. Great severity was used with all such Nonconformists whenever the bishops and creatures of the court could lay hold of them. But they met their fate with undaunted courage. "There was a spirit of uncommon zeal in these people," says the historian, "to suffer all extremities for the cause in which they were engaged."* Heavy fines, cruel and long imprisonments, in which they were often herded with felons, and exposed to the inclemency of the weather, and to noisome pestilential vapours; the pillory, and even death, were the means used to compel the Dissenters to conform to the usages of the Church by law established. But persecution only cherished the resolution it sought to crush. In one of their letters, the writer, a layman, says: "The reason why we will not hear our parish ministers is because they will not stand forth, and defend the Gospel against the leavings of Popery, for fear of loss of goods, or punishment of body, or

* Neal, I. chap. v. p. 219.

danger of imprisonment, or else for fear of men more than God. . . . Awake, oh! ye cold and lukewarm preachers, out of sleep! gird up yourselves with truth; come forth and put your necks to the yoke, and think with Peter that persecution is no strange thing. . . . Let us never fear death, which is conquered by Christ, but believe in him and live for ever."*

" Great numbers of the people," we are told, " being now excluded (by the Act of Uniformity) from the churches, which they could not attend without receiving more offence than benefit, came to a resolution (1566) though with much reluctance, to separate from the Church, lay aside the English Liturgy, and use the Geneva Service-book." †

Commissions were issued immediately after the Act of Uniformity was passed, and visitors at once appointed to carry its persecuting provisions into effect; but in the midst of all this opposition from the Queen and her advisers, the Puritans gained ground. The press was of course restrained, but nevertheless, " great service was rendered by pamphlets privately printed and circulated." At length, after thirteen years of incessant and harrassing persecution, we find a systematic and organized movement commenced for the establishment of a free Christian Church, or society in which the true Head of the Church Universal should alone be recognized as supreme. The results, by the blessing of God, are with us to this day.

Let us then transport ourselves back in the history of our country nearly 300 years. On the 20th November, 1572, you behold two or three boats full of staid personages, of sombre dress, but of devout aspect and resolute will, ascending the mighty river that flows through the metropolis. Probably they were enveloped in a fog. But the light of God's blessing was shining in their hearts. "At a village on its banks, called Wandsworth, five miles from the city," you see them step ashore, and wending their way quietly, so as not to excite observation, they meet divers puritan and dissatisfied brethren who have come on horse-

* Neal, I. chap. v., p. 219.   † See Neal I. iv., p. 205.

back or a-foot, in a humble building,* standing in a yard out of the principal street. A presbytery is then and there chosen, consisting of eleven elders, and as you gaze upon the scene you behold the first Presbyterian Church, nay, the first regularly organized Dissenting Church formed in England. The 20th November, 1572. A day deserving to be had in remembrance by all who honour devoted adherence to the Word of God, rather than slavish conformity to the spiritual despotism of man—to be remembered by those especially who may glory in being the representatives of this noble Presbyterian Nonconformity.

" The heads of the Association were Mr. Field, lecturer of Wandsworth, Mr. Smith, of Mitcham, Mr. Crane, of Roehampton, [clergymen], Messrs. Willcox, Standen, Jackson, Bonham, Saintloe, and Edwards, to whom were afterwards joined Messrs. Travers, Chake, Barber, Gardiner, Crook, Egerton, and a number of very considerable laymen." The offices of the eleven elders above mentioned, were described in a register entitled, " the orders of Wandsworth." " All imaginable care was taken to keep their proceedings secret, but the bishop's eye was upon them, who gave immediate intelligence to the *High Commission*, upon which the Queen issued out a proclamation for putting the Act of Uniformity in execution ; but though the Commissioners knew of the presbytery, they could not discover the members of it, nor prevent others from being erected in neighbouring counties." †

Such was the first systematic commencement of dissent on English soil. But in order to judge of the stress under which these men thus separated themselves from the existing Church, we ought to have some idea of the melancholy condition to which that church, and the people who looked to it for religious nourishment, were reduced. Bishop Sandys, in a sermon before the Queen, tells her Majesty, " That many of her people, especially in the northern parts, perished for want of saving food. Many there

* According to tradition, the present venerable Independent Chapel stands upon the very site of that honoured edifice.

† Neal, vol. I., chap. v., p. 266.

are (says he) that hear not a sermon in seven years, I might safely say in seventeen. Their blood will be required at somebody's hands."* Neal says that many churches were shut up in London for want of ministers, and affecting illustrations of the state of things are given by him and Strype, as well as in the biographies of Grindal, Parker, &c. The University of Cambridge, which had the power of licensing twelve clergymen independently of the bishops, " made use of their privilege to the relief of the Puritans † ;" but the Archbishop called in all licenses over which he had control, and great numbers of the clergy were deprived of their incumbencies, and cast into prison. " The cries of the people reached the court; the secretary wrote to the Archbishop [Parker] to supply the churches, and release the prisoners. But his Grace was inexorable." ‡

Under these circumstances, and from these causes, then, English Presbyterianism took its rise. Many of the evils of which the Puritans complained may seem to us trifling, and their scruples without cause. But it must not be forgotten that the outward form, against which they protested at the cost of so much suffering, were all symbolic acts that to their mind and conscience expressed idolatrous disloyalty to God. § Their resistance was the obeying conscience and God rather than man, and was at once a vindication of the honour of God, the supremacy of Christ, and the authority of the Bible against Popes, Councils, Prelates, and Kings. The occasion of the resistance may sometimes have been puerile and unimportant, but the penalties of protesting were anything but trifling, and in proportion to the severity of their sufferings, and the greatness of their sacrifices, was the heroism and piety called forth. We may be, we *ought* to be, proud of our ancestors. If we revere the memory of those who gained the Great Charter of English political freedom on the plains of Runnymede, far deeper should be our reverence

* Life of Grindal, p. 99. Pierce, p. 52. Quoted by Neal, vol. I, ch. iv, p. 198.

† Neal, p. 195.   ‡ Neal, I., vol. i. p. 198.

§ See Neal, I., p. p. 521, 522, (Editor's Notes.)

for those who, at infinitely greater cost, and by the nobler weapons of Christian protest, struggled for our religious rights and liberties. But it was the same profound instincts, the same thirst for freedom, and hatred of tyranny in every form, that has always inspired English hearts to resist alike political and ecclesiastical oppression, and made our history memorable. Wickliffe and the Lollards, in this respect, were the spiritual ancestors of the English Presbyterians. *They* first, in this country, strove to break the yoke of bondage wherewith papal Rome held the heritage of Christ in slavery. A blessed era of religious liberty appeared to be dawning on the English nation in the reign of Edward VI., years after Wickliffe and the martyrs of his age had gone to their honoured graves. And then when that light was over-clouded, and the prayers and blood of the first Reformers seemed to have been almost in vain, arose the Puritans of England and Scotland. A nobler race of men, according to their light, has seldom struggled for righteousness and truth. They were the worthy successors of Wickliffe and Lord Cobham; and English Presbyterianism was the earliest, and for nearly two centuries the most efficient form of Puritan organization and zeal until the Act of Toleration, under Wm. III.

Let it then be clearly understood that English Presbyterianism in its origin was essentially a vindication of the rights of the human soul, a principle of resistance to priestcraft and ecclesiastical tyranny, for the sake of preserving allegiance to God and his revealed Truth. It was not resistance for political and social purposes, still less from impatience of restraint, or merely human indignation against oppression. It was a determined effort on the part of certain English Christians in the 16th century, to stand fast in the liberty wherewith they felt that *Christ* had made them free. In the words of Mr. Tayler, " The fundamental idea of Puritanism in all its forms and ramifications, is the supreme authority of Scripture, acting directly on the individual conscience as opposed to a reliance on the priesthood, and the outward ordinances of the Church. To realize the standard of faith, worship, and conduct recorded in Scripture, has ever been the object of Puritanism ; and to attain that object in defiance of a hierarchy, requires no small degree of self-reliance and decision of purpose."* It required also no small measure of piety, of faith in things unseen, in divine promises and divine help, no faint spirit of devotedness to God and his Christ, to Truth and Duty. Hence Puritanism while originating in these noble and all-important qualities, in turn re-acted on the religious life of the Puritans, and cherished the faith, piety, and godliness for which they were so remarkable.

In another passage, the same writer observes, " Puritanism, which from its origin was rather a product and expression of popular feeling, than the impulse of a speculative intellect, casting off by a spasmodic effort the constraint and oppression of the old sacerdotal yoke, threw itself with implicit trust on Scripture, as a substituted authority; and opposed the claims of God and Christ to those of uninspired and erring men. The idea was grand and animating."* And again, "Thus the sufficiency of Scripture is the fundamental postulate of Puritanism; the authority of the Church, the ground practically taken by the Anglican hierarchy ; and these incompatible assumptions have been the cause of the unintermitted strife between them through the last four or five centuries of our history. Scripture, the record and depository of the free and popular spirit of the primitive Gospel, the Magna Charta of religious liberty, is a standing witness and protest against the pretensions of spiritual despotism." †

These then being the great fundamental principles to which English Presbyterianism owed its birth, we shall not be surprised to find that the particular form of Church Government from which it takes its name, has always held a very subordinate place in the affections of English Presbyterians. And when we inquire how their dissent from the established church happened to take this form, we find it was owing to the circumstances in which the English Protestants were placed during Queen Mary's Reign of Terror. It was Genevan influence which moulded English Nonconformity in its infancy. The numerous exiles who fled from the Marian persecution found a refuge, some at the birthplace of Calvinism in the cradle of civic as well as religious liberty, Switzerland, some at Frankfort-on-the-Maine. There they enjoyed the blessings

* Retrospect, &c., p. 88, 2nd Edit.   † Retrospect, &c., p. 89.

which were denied them in their father-land, and there they became introduced to Presbyterianism. It was during Mary's reign, and at Frankfort, that the first English congregation was formed abroad. But instead of adopting King Edward's service-book without alteration they used neither the litany nor surplice, and agreed to employ the service-book "so far as God's word commanded." Hence this may be considered as in reality the first congregation established by English separatists from the Church of England. They met with great opposition from those exiles who remained thorough-going adherents to King Edward's service-book, and being rather unfairly dealt with by them, at length removed to Geneva, where they had the celebrated John Knox and a Mr. Goodman for their pastors. Here they formally adopted the Genevan discipline, service, and liturgy ; and hence, when under Queen Elizabeth's oppressive measures they were compelled to forsake the church in which they had been brought up, we can under-stand their adopting that form of Church Government with which they had become acquainted during their exile, and which was there commended to their judgment by the example of Calvin and Knox. The sympathy they met with from the Protestants of Geneva not only developed their love of freedom and devotedness to Scripture, but naturally led them to perceive a greater authority in the Bible for the Presbyterianism of their pious and hospitable friends abroad, than for the despotic prelacy of their oppressors at home. But so far was Presby-terianism from striking deep root in English Puritan soil, or from ever becoming a fundamental principle with English Presbyterians, that even the closing years of Queen Elizabeth's reign, we find it recorded, "were marked by a decline of zeal for the proper Presbyterian discipline." "To this change of public feeling," it is said, "various causes may have contributed ; the experience of their utter inability to overturn or materially alter the existing establishments ; a more learned and candid appreciation of the Scriptural evidence on which either Presbyterianism or Episcopacy was alleged to stand ; the rapid spread of principles which took a bolder view, and had as little respect for Presbyterianism, as a national system upheld by the State, as for Episcopacy ; and the tranquilizing expectation of ecclesiastical reform from the [approaching] accession of a Presbyterian sovereign to the throne."* Neal, also, remarks on the decline of zeal for Presbyterianism twenty years before the breaking out of the civil wars. And although it received a temporary stimulus from the alliance of the Scotch Covenanters with the English Puritans, and even became the national established form of Church government during the Commonwealth, as will be presently noticed, yet there is a great amount of evidence to prove that the interest of English Presbyterians in this particular form of ecclesiastical organisation was never very strong and always subordinate from the very first to those main principles set forth above. Hence a minister of the English Presbyterians at the present day, preaching before the Provincial Assembly of Presbyterian Ministers of Lancashire and Cheshire on their 210th anniversary, at Liverpool, June 21st, 1855 (the Rev. R. L. Carpenter), could say with truth, "Presbyterian is our family name; it does not describe an accident of our conformation †, but recalls our origin and kindred; it unites us by no bond of opinion or discipline, but as a household of Christian faith." The Presbyterian form of Church government never having been an essential of English Presbyterianism, the name has long been used, and may with perfect correctness continue to be used in the way above expressed, though no Presbyterian government is exercised among those who bear it.

The Presbyterian system having, however, been introduced into this country, and partially organised in 1572, according to the account above given, it appears to have been hailed by numbers of earnest men as a refuge from the iron rule and Popish practices of the Established Church. It is not proposed, of course, in the present sketch to follow the history of the English Presbyterians through the 300 years which have nearly elapsed since that first formation of a Presbytery at Wandsworth in 1572, but simply to glance at the leading facts and principles in that history, and to share the results which have remained to the present day. Suffice it then to say, that after their

* Retrospect, &c., p. p. 109, 110.

† i. e., not of our modern conformation; but it does indicate, as shown above, the accident that led to its original adoption in the 16th century.

thus becoming a distinct religious society, they continued to gain strength and numbers in spite—or, perhaps we ought to say with the help of severe persecution—until we find them wielding a mighty power in the State and the Church during the reign of Charles I., and leading the war in the terrible struggles of that period for emancipation from political and ecclesiastical tyranny. For those were the palmy days of English Presbyterians, when they rose to great heights of influence, and shone conspicuous alike in the Senate, and in the conferences of the Church. Then also we behold them flaming forth with noble indignation against the faithlessness of their oppressors, and shedding their blood in many a deadly fight, until the freedom of their country was achieved, and that work virtually accomplished which continental nations are even now vainly striving to do themselves, or to get done for them, lest they utterly perish. The Long Parliament which, with all its errors, was the noblest and devoutest body of men that ever met in this, or perhaps in any other country, to achieve the liberties of a nation, was mainly composed of our English Presbyterian forefathers. So also was the Westminster Assembly of divines.* And the bulk of those victorious troops who withstood the fiery charge of Rupert's Cavaliers, and finally broke the military power of the Crown, consisted of the same material. Of the piety, wisdom, and valour of the Independents, and the important part they also played in these eventful struggles, this is not the place to speak. It is sufficient to remark, that while numerically far inferior to the Presbyterians, and also in weight of influence as a body, they numbered in their ranks some of the noblest minds of the day, and exercised a proportionate power; while in general appreciation of the principles of religious liberty, they were then far in advance of the Presbyterians. † Would that they had retained in later days when

* Some of the Episcopal clergy appointed by Parliament never attended, and nearly all the rest withdrew soon after its sittings commenced. There were only about six Independent ministers, and a few Erastians belonging to it, but no Baptists.

† See their protest in the Westminster Assembly through Philip Nye and others. Also Leonard Busher's Treatise on Religious Peace, 1614.

B

their relative position with regard to Presbyterians had changed, the same loyalty to the rights of the human soul which distinguished them when they stood fearless in the presence of overwhelming majorities of men whose bigotry was too often in proportion to the intensity of their devotion to what they believed to be the cause of God.

But with all their faults, never let it for a moment be doubted or forgotten that the Presbyterians of England, in the days of Charles I. and Cromwell, as well as in earlier times, were a body of men such as the best and wisest of her sons delight to honour. Speaking of the Westminster Assembly and the Long Parliament, the historian before quoted says with equal insight and beauty :—" Such a spectacle had never before been witnessed in England, neither has there been any repetition of it since. Of all who were interested in the canse of freedom, civil and religious, and who had dared the last extremity in asserting it, the wisest, gravest and best were now convened in solemn amity, to seek by their united counsels and endeavours in Parliament and the Assembly, the two highest objects embraced in the social well-being of man : just and equal government, and such provision for moral and spiritual culture as would secure its perpetuity in a race of virtuous and high-principled freemen. They seemed now to be approaching the end, which the truest patriots had sought through the dark and blood-stained contingencies of civil discord; and some perhaps were already anticipating a long era of peace and glory for their country. If in looking back on their undertaking from our more elevated point of view, we discern in the conditions of human society, insuperable obstacles to its successful accomplishment, we ought not to be insensible to the patriotic motives which prompted it; nor while we deplore that perverted earnestness which often took the form of intolerance, to overlook the patient thoughtfulness, the strong religious conviction, and the high moral purpose, which have conferred an immortal reputation on many of the acts of the Long Parliament, and leave no small praise due to the intentions and efforts of the Assembly. The great and good men of this greatest period in our national history, attempted in the largeness of their patriotism, directed by views which were then all but universal, to combine objects hitherto found incompatible ; to blend good government and civil freedom in one compact and harmonious fabric, with a fixed type of faith and worship for the entire nation. Most of them seem not to have suspected, that a denial of the fundamental principles of the Reformation was contained in their design."*

No, they still saw but through a glass darkly on these vital questions of the right of private judgment and the relation of religion to the state. It cost them and their descendants many years of persecution under the restored Stuarts, and of enlightened training under men like Baxter and Henry, before they understood the true principles of religious liberty ; but their earnestness and piety, their devoted self-sacrificing zeal and faithfulness, these remain as a very precious memory, for all who can value it.

On the 6th of June, 1646, the English Presbyterians may be said to have reached the culminating point of their political glory, for on that day a bill passed the House of Lords, which had been carried in the Commons some months before, formally establishing Presbyterianism as the system of government for the national Church of England. The provisions of the Act were, however, fully carried out only in Middlesex and Lancashire, and partly in Devonshire, which, as fourteen years elapsed before the Restoration, is a corroboration of the statement that the interest of English Presbyterians, in the Presbyterian mode of government has never been very energetic. The Presbyterian clergy, however, were inducted in great numbers into those benefices of which their forefathers had been to so great an extent deprived in the reign of Elizabeth, and they found themselves once more exercising the ministry for which they had been trained at the national Universities, in the bosom of that church from which their fathers had so sorrowfully seceded, or been so violently expelled.

We must not conceal from ourselves that this period of Presbyterian power and prosperity was disgraced by some

* Retrospect, pp. 131, 132.

grievous displays of bigotry and intolerance, a full account of which will be found in Neal's History (vol. iv., chap. 1, &c.). "Toleration" they believed to be a fatal delusion of the devil, and contemptuously termed it the "Great Diana" of the Independents. The ordinance against Blasphemy and Heresy must especially be noticed. It "enacted that for certain specified offences under this head, if the party should not abjure his error, or if having abjured he should relapse, he should suffer death, as in case of felony without benefit of clergy." "This," says Neal, "is one of the most shocking laws I have met with in restraint of religious liberty,"* but it was not passed without much opposition,† and as Mr. Tayler observes, "under the sharp stimulus of hatred to the various sects with which the vicinity of the army had recently annoyed them."‡ We must remember also the terribly harassed state of men's minds at this period, the wild license of speculation, and the distracting hopes and fears which agitated the leading men of every sect. Happily owing to the disturbed state of the times the act proved a mere *brutum fulmen,* and was never carried into effect.

On the death of Cromwell, the Presbyterian party manifested an unequivocal desire for the restoration of Charles Stuart, provided the requisite guarantees could be obtained for those reforms of the rubric and liturgy for which they and their Puritan ancestors had suffered and striven so long. These guarantees were given by Charles, at Breda, in April, 1660, at the earnest solicitation of the Presbyterians, promising to grant "liberty to tender consciences, and that no man shall be disquieted or called in question for differences of opinion in matters of religion, which do not disturb the peace of the kingdom."§ Behold the deputation returning triumphant from their interview with the son of their dethroned and beheaded monarch,‖ looking forward with devout thankfulness to many years of peaceful labours in the Church of Christ, in which

* Neal, III, ch. x, p. p. 458, 9.

† See Whitlock's Memor. p. 302.   ‡ Retrospect, p. 147, Note.

§ Neal, IV, ch. iv, p. 251. This declaration he afterwards solemnly confirmed.

‖ Not that all things went quite to their satisfaction even at Breda. See Neal IV, p. 253.

they should be united in amicable compromise with their episcopal brethren, under the mild and tolerant rule of the young sovereign thus about to be welcomed home to the throne of his fathers. Whatever we may think of the wisdom of the leading Presbyterian divines at this juncture (and it is easy to be wise after the event!), there can be no doubt as to the conciliatory and Christian spirit in which such men as Reynolds,* Spurstow, Baxter, Calamy, and others, were labouring to effect a settlement of ecclesiastical affairs that should " keep the unity of the spirit in the bond of peace." They willingly concurred in the return of the episcopal party to power, and in the modified re-establishment of episcopacy,† believing that both those measures would promote that religious liberty and that union of the two great parties in the Church which they so cordially desired. But success is not always granted to noble purpose and earnest effort.

Sir Matthew Hale's bill for making the "Declaration" of the King (repeating his promise made at Breda) into law, was lost in the House of Commons‡ (Nov. 28, 1660,) by a majority of twenty-six. A little later, (April 15, in the following year), twenty-one Episcopalian, and the same number of Presbyterian clergymen, assembled according to the King's Declaration of Oct. 25, to hold a conference at the Bishop of London's lodgings at the Savoy in the Strand, with the professed object of seeing if some arrangements could not be made for "the restoring and continuance of peace and unity in the churches under his Majesty's government and direction" by making "such reasonable and necessary alterations, corrections, and amendments [in ' the book of common prayer'] as shall be agreed upon to be needful, and expedient for giving satisfaction to tender consciences,"§ But the Presbyterians, (whose petitions were singularly moderate), soon found to their sorrow that there was no real

---

* Dr. Reynolds was vice-chancellor of Oxford, and dean of Christ Church. He was one of the few Presbyterian Divines who conformed at the Restoration, when he accepted the Bishopric of Norwich.

† Neal, IV, chap. v, p. 292.

‡ Elected under reactionary influences, often of the worst description.

§ "Declaration," quoted by Neal, IV, ch. vi, p. 237.

intention on the side of the Church party to endeavour to remove the obstacles to union, and that "nothing more was intended than to drop the Presbyterians with decency." Archbishop Usher's recommendations were not to be thought of, and they were forbidden to claim even the concessions promised in the King's late declaration. Of course, the conference led to no result.

There are few more sorrowful chapters in English history than that which records the stealthy, treacherous, tiger-like steps by which the High Church and Tory party gradually crept in upon their helpless victims after the King's return, and at length made their fatal spring in the shape of another Act of Uniformity, more celebrated and more cruel than Queen Elizabeth's, with all the added infamy of broken vows and basest ingratitude. By this disgraceful statute, which, through a singular fatality, that profligate monarch, Charles II., has linked for ever with the memory of the atrocious massacre of St. Bartholomew in France, all ministers of religion were required to give their "unfeigned assent and consent to all and every thing contained and prescribed in and by the Book of Common Prayer,"* before "the feast of St. Bartholomew," August 24, 1662, under pain of being deprived of their livings, and being disabled from preaching. Should they attempt to preach while so disabled, they were to suffer three months' imprisonment for every offence. "Every minister was also required to renounce his Presbyterian ordination. . . . No provision was made for those who would not comply with these terms, though both Queen Elizabeth and Cromwell allowed one-fifth of the benefice for the maintenance of the ejected incumbent." And this was the treatment received by the very men through whose instrumentality the King had been replaced on the throne, and his Bishops on the bench. But however sad for those who committed this great wrong, the consequences to our Presbyterian ancestors, like the consequences of many another wrong,—even such a one as that of Calvary,—were signally blessed to the sufferers. "Through much tribulation" they rose to heights of self-sacrifice and holy heroism, and ultimately attained to a spirit of Christian enlightened and large-hearted charity, which they never could

* Neal, ch. vi., p. p. 372, 373.

have won without passing through that fire-baptism of suffering. The result of that Act of Uniformity is well known, and will not soon be forgotten. Two thousand Presbyterian clergymen, pious, devoted, noble-hearted men, nearly all of them graduates of Oxford or Cambridge, regularly ordained, as well as educated, for the exercise of their sacred calling,*—on that memorable day gave up their beloved churches and pleasant houses rather than conform to what their consciences forbad ; and without any certain means of livelihood, went forth bearing their cross, ready to suffer all things for the sake of their allegiance to Christ. Very grievous, says Neal, "were the calamities of far the greater part of these unhappy sufferers, who, with their families, must have perished, if private collections in London, and divers places of the country, had not been made for their subsistence."† "The people they left were not able to relieve them, nor durst they if they had been able, because it would have been called a maintenance of schism or faction. Many of the ministers being afraid to lay down their ministry after they had been ordained to it, preached to such as would hear them, in fields and private houses, till they were apprehended and cast into gaols where many of them perished. The people were no less divided ; some conformed, and others were driven to a greater distance from the church, and resolved to abide by their faithful pastors at all events. They murmured at the Government, and called the bishops and conforming clergy cruel persecutors ; for which and for their frequenting the private assemblies of their ministers, they were fined and imprisoned, till many families left their native country and settled in the plantations"(of America.‡) The ejected ministers were ridiculed on the stage, and mobbed by the rabble in the streets. "Such magistrates were put into commission as executed the penal laws with severity. Informers were encouraged and rewarded. It is impossible to relate the number of the sufferings both of ministers and people; the great trials, with hardships upon their persons, estates, and families, by uncomfortable separations, dispersions,

* Bishoprics were offered to several of the leading Presbyterian divines by the Government, on condition of conformity.

† vol. iv., ch. vi., p. 388.

‡ Baxter's Life, part ii., page 385, quoted by Neal.

unsettlements and removes; disgraces, reproaches, imprisonments, chargeable journies, expenses in law, tedious sickness, and innumerable diseases ending in death; great disquietments and frights to the wives and families, and their doleful effects upon them."* "This [ejectment]," says Calamy, " was an action without a precedent: the like to this, the Reformed Church, nay the Christian world, never saw before." " This Act of Uniformity was passed in a heat, but its effects have been dreadful and lasting. So that we may well, (and I hope without offence,) drop a tear upon the remembrance of so many worthies in our Israel, who were buried at once in a common grave."†

We must not pursue at greater length the fate of our forefathers during their quarter of a century of persecution and suffering. It is enough to remind their descendants that in the reign of Charles II. alone, nearly 8,000 Protestant Dissenters perished in prison;‡ and within the compass of only three years they suffered pecuniary loss in trade, fines, &c., to to the amount of at least £2,000,000 sterling. The names of 60,000 Dissenters were collected, who suffered in one way or other on account of their religion, between the Restoration and and the Revolution; and their pecuniary losses during that period, at a moderate computation, amounted to £12 or £14,000,000 sterling § About the same number of persons are computed to have suffered during the three preceding reigns. Truly, there is a very solemn utterance coming from those desolate homes and noisome jails to us who tranquilly repose under the shadow of that tree of Religious Liberty and Peace, which our fathers planted in sorrow and watered with their tears. It is a very serious question what God may reasonably expect of us who inherit with their principles, memory, and name, the rights and duties for which they strove so nobly and suffered so deeply. It has been said that they went

* Conformist Plea for the Non-conformist, part iv., p. 40, quoted by Neal.

† Nonconformists' Memorial," vol. i, p. 33., Palmer's editn., 1775.

‡ The Five-mile Act, and the Act against Conventicles, filled the jails with Dissenters, and were the principal instruments of persecution. The pillory was not seldom resorted to.

§ Neal, vol. v., ch. i., p. p. 21, 22.

more cheerfully to prison than their descendants to public worship, and paid their ruinous fines more willingly than we contribute some infinitesimal portion of our income to the upholding and extending of the Church of Christ. However this may be, we know, nevertheless, there is much true-hearted devotedness, thank God! much genuine self-sacrifice among us still. Our forefathers had no Sunday or Ragged Schools, no missions to the Heathen, or to the neglected poor of our large towns. But we know that worldly peace and prosperity are more dangerous than adversity, and that the mightiest States as well as the proudest Churches have fallen in the day of luxurious tranquillity, when they had withstood the fiercest assaults, nay, even grown and flourished amid the persecutions, of sterner times. Had the Dissenters' Chapels Bill not passed the Legislature,* there would probably have been such a manifesta-of religious life and zeal among the Presbyterian descendants of the ejected ministers as England has not witnessed since the days of Wesley. If a Ministers' Stipend Augmentation Fund of £30,000 be the consequence of the one great unrighteous victory gained over us in the Lady Hewley suit, what might not have been the amount of generous self-sacrificing zeal called forth by 200 such victories?

Yet it is but an inferior and certainly a torpid form of piety and benevolence that requires persecution to goad it into active life. Shall we not serve God and our Saviour through gratitude alone? Woe to us if we allow the mercies of our Heavenly Father to wean our affections *from* Him, or to lessen our sacrifices *to* Him. He has protected us in the rightful possession of our chapels, endowments, and religious liberties. He has brought us, and the generations now gathered to their rest, out of the Egyptian darkness and bondage of the days of the Tudors and Stuarts. Must we be led back from the Promised Land, and "overthrown in the wilderness," because with many of us "God is not well-pleased"?

We must now glance briefly at the fortunes of our Presbyterian ancestors subsequent to the memorable Revolution which wrought out so great a deliverance for this country, and are accordingly directed by the progress of their history to observe a very noble characteristic of English Presbyterianism, which

* In 1844.

was developed under the pressure of persecution into ripened and fruitful forms, and which had always been a marked feature in its character. I mean the fervent longing of the English Presbyterians from the time of Queen Elizabeth to the present day for a truly Catholic Church. They have always longed for and believed in the possibility of a National Church, which should comprehend the sincere and devout among all Christian sects. There have indeed been sorrowful exceptions in their history to this large-hearted charity; and in the earlier periods of that history, of course it was restricted by the prevalent views of Christian Communion; while throughout it has, (equally of course,) not been wholly independent of the influences of the age. But after making all necessary allowances, the great fact still shines out with unquestionable distinctness, that these honoured men did yearn for a broad comprehensive Christian union—did earnestly desire to have as little of sectarian division as faithfulness to Scripture and conscience would permit—that they never indulged in schism and dissent for the sake of separation, nor separated from their brethren of the Establishment except with sorrow and pain. We have become so much accustomed in these days to Dissent and Sectarianism, it is so associated with our reverence for the rights of conscience that some of us perhaps can hardly realize the intense longing of our Puritan ancestors for a united church. They became Dissenters only when conformity outraged their highest principles.* And indeed do not all men in proportion as they are in earnest about Religion, seeking the glory of God, not their own, the establishment of Christ's dominion rather than of their own sect or party, do they not desire Christian union? Do they not know that in division there is always weakness, that united effort is essential to vigorous action? And especially do they not feel the deep blessing of religious sympathy and Christian communion? The more men's hearts are filled with the love of God, the more do they desire to live in peace and love with

* A striking illustration of this fact is the remark of Oliver Heywood concerning his father-in-law, the Rev. John Angier, in his memoir of that devout and noble-hearted man,—"He had Catholic principles, and loved *aliquid Christi*, anything of Christ, wherever he saw it, and continued the good old Puritan spirit to his dying day."—Quoted by the Rev. R. B. Aspland, in the Re-opening of the Old Chapel, Dukinfield, Oct. 1845.

their brethren, and the more conscious they are of their own spiritual needs and spiritual weakness, the more they desire to enjoy that Christian fellowship and Church Union which is so mighty a help to godliness of heart and life. The converse of the proposition holds good also, and the longing for union generally indicates religious life. Hence we justly regard this marked tendency in the Presbyterian body to seek for a true Catholic Christian Church, as a favourable indication of their Christian aspirations, and a fact most honourable to them as a body of Christian disciples, especially considering the intense sectarianism of the age. But it necessarily detracted from their zeal for the Presbyterian form of Church Government, and is the secret of most of those movements they made at various times towards reunion with the established Church.

The current of events has now floated us down to the period when we have to observe the character and influence of a man who was pre-eminently a representative of English Presbyterians, and of whom their descendants may most justly be proud. I mean Richard Baxter, than whom a more devout, large-hearted Christian Minister never entered a pulpit. This man laboured earnestly to promote a unity of spirit and organization, when the general break-up of existing parties at the time of the Restoration appeared to offer a suitable opening for such endeavours. The following interesting passage is extracted from the MSS., Baxter in Dr. Williams' Library:—" On this occasion, Mr. Baxter becoming acquainted with the bishop (Usher), at last he treated with him about the necessary terms of concord between the Episcopal Divines and the Presbyterians and such other Nonconformists; for you must know that in Worcestershire they had before attempted and agreed upon an association, in which the Episcopal, Presbyterians, Independents, and the disengaged, consented to terms of love and concord in the practising of so much of discipline in their parishes as all the parties were agreed in (which was drawn up), and forbearing each other in the rest. Westmoreland and Cumberland, Essex and Hampshire, and Wiltshire and Dorsetshire quickly imitated them, and made the like association, and it was going on and likely to have been commonly practised till the return of the Bishops after broke it. Mr. Baxter at the same time treated with Bishop

Browning and Dr. Hammond about the terms of the desired concord. But Bishop Usher and he did most speedily agree."*

In the committee appointed in 1654, " to decide upon the fundamentals of Christianity mentioned in the ' Instruments of Government,' the Independent divines, under the guidance of Owen and Thomas Goodwin, produced a formidable list of articles, which would have excluded all who were not Trinitarian and Calvinists." † But Baxter proposed that no more than the Lord's Prayer, the Apostles' Creed, and the Ten Commandments, should be offered to Parliament, " as the Essentials or Fundamentals of Christianity, which at least contain all that is necessary to salvation, and hath been by all eminent churches taken for the sum of their religion ; and whereas it was said 'A Socinian or a Papist will subscribe all this,' I answered, ' So much the better, and so much the fitter it is to be a matter of our concord ; but if you are afraid of communion with Papists and Socinians, it must not be avoided by making a new rule or test of faith which they will not subscribe to, or by forcing others to subscribe to more than they can do, but by calling them to account, whenever in preaching or writing they contradicted or abused the truth to which they here subscribed." ‡

In the Savoy Conferences, of 1661, above referred to, we find the same desire, on the part of the Presbyterians, for peace and union. " A little concession," says a learned writer, " by the High Church party at this time, would have prevented much of that dissension with which they have ever since contended. A union with an able and learned body of persons [the Presbyterians] would have been effected." § By this time the term " Presbyterian "

* Monthly Repository, vol. xx, p. 287, quoted by Mr. Tayler.

† Retrospect, p. 141.

‡ Second part of a Reply to the "Vindication of the Non-subscribing Ministers." See Calamy's Abridgement of the Life of Baxter, 1713, 8 vol., p. 121:

§ The History, Opinions, and Present Legal Position of the English Presbyterians." London, 1834. Page 10. (Drawn up, I believe, by the Rev. Joseph Hunter, a very high authority.)

had quite "ceased to denote exclusive attachment to that form of church government, but embraced all who were not from principle Separatists," (such as the Independents and Baptists) "and who desired a national settlement of religion on the broad basis of purification and reform." A glorious opportunity for the establishment of Christian liberty and unity, was, however, then thrown away by the bigotry and folly of the High Church party and the treachery of Charles II. "There was at that time," says Mr. Tayler, "a deep religious awakening of the human spirit, and a disposition in the best minds on all sides to coalesce in a broad and noble catholicism, such as had never existed before, and of which there has been no revival since. It was the momentary gleam of a better day, soon darkened over again by a cloud of bigotry and intolerance thicker than ever. It was one of those lost opportunities of the past of which history furnishes so mournful a catalogue." *

A bishopric was offered to Baxter by Charles on his restoration, but declined "until the Church should have been put on such a footing as would accord with his sense of Christian principle." With all his large-hearted liberality, Baxter combined "a scrupulous honesty, and sensitive tenderness of conscience."† There was no cringing worldliness, or weak amiable faithlessness to great principles, in that noble heart.

From 1662 to 1688, the English Presbyterians necessarily conducted their affairs on Independent principles. "The persecution to which they were exposed would have rendered it impracticable or imprudent " ‡ to have attempted carrying out their Presbyterian discipline. And when, many years later, the Toleration Act would have allowed of such an organization, their interest in Presbyterianism, which, as we have seen, was never a vital question with them, had altogether died away.

After the Revolution we find our forefathers, however, once more striving for the largest measure of Christian freedom and association. On the accession of Wm. III. to

---

* Retrospect, p. 213. Note.   † Retrospect, p. 150.
‡ History, Opinions, &c., p. 11.

the throne, the Dissenters united in presenting an address, suggesting the widest possible basis for toleration or comprehension, and praying " that the rule of Christianity might be the rule of Conformity."* Endeavours were made and chiefly supported by Dr Tillotson, to meet the Presbyterians half way, in reference to which Calamy, himself a representative Presbyterian, remarks, " I was one of those that was very well disposed towards falling in with the Establishment, could his (Dr. Tillotson's) scheme have taken effect." Hallam, in his Constitutional History of England, remarks on the higher ground which the Presbyterians by this time had fully occupied in reference to religious freedom. " The motives of Dissent," says he, " were already somewhat changed, and came to turn less on the petty scruples of the elder Puritans, than on a dislike to all subscriptions of faith, and compulsory uniformity." † Even after Tillotson's measures had failed, we find that many of the Presbyterians " occasionally communicated with the [State] Church, to show their love of peace and charity, their desire for union, and their wish to avoid what was considered as the sin of schism." ‡ Calamy, who was certainly one of the most illustrious of the Presbyterian divines of the 17th and 18th centuries, both as a preacher and writer, and Peirce, of Exeter, who was also a distinguished minister, have recorded these views for themselves and others. John Howe, chaplain to Cromwell, one of the greatest ornaments of the Presbyterian body, and the contemporary of Baxter, is another bright example of this Christian catholic spirit. §

The gradual developement of the great principle of English Presbyterianism in another very interesting and important direction, now demands our attention.

It has been well remarked that the same spirit of resistance to ecclesiastical tyranny, the same devoted zeal for

* Address to the Crown, quoted in the " History, Opinions, &c.," pp. 13, 14.

† Hallam, Const. History, vol. III., p. 237.　‡ History, &c., p. 16.

§ See, among many other striking remarks by Howe, a quotation from Calamy, in the " Retrospect," p. 310.

religious liberty and the rights of conscience which led the earlier Presbyterians to defend their freedom against Elizabeth, Parker, Laud, and the Stuarts, prompted them in the 18th century to assert the rights of each individual soul against the spiritual despotism of their fellow Dissenters, the Independents and Baptists. The Independents in their earlier days, when they were the weaker body, had more than once, as we have seen, set a noble example, and read a severe lesson to the Presbyterians, when these were untrue to their own principles. But as the former grew in strength, they increased in bigotry, and in their turn played the traitor to the great principles of Puritanism and Protestantism. But the Presbyterians at length learned in the school of trial, and under the influence of such men as Baxter, Calamy, and Howe, the height, and breadth, and depth of the glorious convictions which had been essentially the animating principles of their forefathers. And thus at the Revolution they had gradually become deeply rooted in a true love of the liberty wherewith they felt Christ had made them and all Christians free. In resisting the attacks and persecution of prelacy they had become trained to resist intolerance and spiritual usurpation wherever they met with it. Hence about the beginning of last century they found themselves brought into collision with their less liberal dissenting brethren.

Many of the eminent Presbyterian clergymen, to whom reference has been made, during the long course of their earnest ministry had gradually receded from the rigid Calvinism of their fathers, while some of the Independents had on the contrary been approaching even the very verge of Antinomianism. This controvery gave rise to a party called Baxterians, and these again went on into decided Arminianism. Hence arose strong jealousies and hostile feelings, on the part of the Calvinistic Dissenters, who endeavoured more strenuously than ever to enforce adhesion to the Westminister Assembly's Confession of Faith. The natural tendency of the most liberal view of God's dealings with man was to encourage a more liberal spirit in men's intercourse and relations with one another. The Presbyterians allowed open communion, while the Independents insisted upon previous inquiries and confessions of faith. In like manner, ever since the Presbyterian Fund was established in London, in 1689, "it has always been a fundamental principle of the Board 'not to require any confession or explanation of faith as a qualification for relief.' "* The Independent or Congregational Board has acted on the contrary principle. Matters were brought to a crisis in the year 1719, a year very memorable in the annals of religious liberty. Mr. Peirce, one of the Presbyterian minister of St. George's Meeting, Exeter, had proclaimed his conversion to Arian opinions, and Mr. Hallett, his colleague occupied much the same position. Dr. Williams, the eminent founder of the Libraries and Charities in Red Cross-street, was violently attacked on charges of heresy, by the Independents, and even his personal character was assailed. These malicious attacks, however, so far from injuring him, only exalted his reputation, but his name was left out of the Pinners' Hall Joint Lecture, and another lecture at Salter's Hall, was consequently established. Emlyn had been prosecuted as early as 1702, for Arian opinions, and the press teemed with Arian and Unitarian publications. "Perhaps at no period," we read, "was the Unitarian controversy so actively carried on as between 1690 and 1720." † This case, however, of Mr. Peirce brought matters to a crisis. Reference was made by the Exeter congregation to the London Dissenting ministers, and conferences were held in Slater's Hall, commencing March 3rd, 1719, for "the full consideration of the affair." After prolonged and animated discussion on a proposition that all persons presenting themselves for ordination should subscribe to a declaration of their belief in the Trinity, there was a majority (principally composed of Presbyterian ministers), against any subscription or confession, of 73 to 69. Many, if not all, of this majority no doubt conscientiously believed the doctrine of the Trinity. But, as it has been well said, "They had separated from the Establishment for conscience sake; for conscience, their ancestors and some of themselves had set the law and

* History and Opinions, &c., p. 19. † Ibid. p. 22.

government at defiance; and should they surrender this liberty, which they had so dearly purchased to men who were only their associates in trial and suffering?" * No! To their eternal honour, and to our infinite gain, and (what is far more important) to the gain of the holy cause of Scriptural truth and religious freedom, they refused to be "again entangled in the yoke of bondage." The children of the Puritans showed themselves worthy of their descent.

A few extracts from the admirable statement by the majority, of their reasons for refusing to establish or sanction any tests and confessions of faith, will be read with interest, but the whole volume relating to the "Salter's Hall Conference," and which may be seen at Dr. Williams' Library, is well deserving of perusal.

Among other replies to the arguments of their opponents "that if we subscribed it would prevent the spreading of erroneous opinions amongst those whom our names might be supposed to influence," they say, after protesting against "any groundless suspicion" of their own unsoundness on the Trinity,—"And we are still fully persuaded that a Faith built upon our authority is a vain thing in itself. We think ourselves obliged often to inculcate this principle upon our hearers, that they ought not to form their judgment in matters necessary to salvation by the private sentiments of their ministers any further than they are supported by the Word of God. And we assure ourselves that a tender and scrupulous regard for the Word of God will never be thought either dangerous or inconvenient to the body of Protestant Dissenters.

" IV. We saw no reason to think that a Declaration in other words than those of Scripture would serve the cause of Peace and Truth; but rather be the occasion of greater confusions and disorders. We have found it always so in history. And, in reason, the words of men appear to us more liable to different interpretations than the words of Scripture; since all may fairly think themseves more at liberty to put their own sense upon Humane forms than upon the words of the Holy Ghost. And in this case what

* History, &c., p. 22.

C

assurance could we have that all who subscribed meant precisely the same sense any more than if they had made a declaration in express words of Scripture. . . . . . .

VII. We take it to be an inverting the great rule of *deciding controversy among Protestants*, making the explication and words of men determine the sense of Scripture instead of making the Scripture to determine how far the words of men are to be regarded. We therefore could not give our hands to do that which in present circumstances would be like to mislead others to set up Humane explications for the *decisive rule* of Faith. We did, and do now, judge it our duty to remonstrate against such a precedent, as opening a way to (what we dread) the most fatal *breaches on gospel liberty*.

" VIII. Though we would not charge our brethren that required our subscriptions with a design which any of them do disclaim, yet to us it appeared, and does still appear, to have the *nature of imposition*; which has been the great engine of division among Christians from the beginning, and has done unspeakable mischief to the Christian Church.

" IX. We thought it would be a reproach upon us to do anything that looked like *giving up our Christian liberty*, when others with so great *strength* of argument are pleading for it.

" X. We foresaw the subscription insisted upon would occasion reflection, and become a mark of distinction set on those who should not subscribe. And we knew that several who had the same faith and opinions concerning the Trinity with ourselves and our brethren, yet could not be satisfied to come into any Humane explications.

" XI. We could not but think it would highly reflect on those among ourselves who had been known often to declare against everything of this nature.

" XII. We observed the enemies of the Protestant Dissenters to be great encouragers and approvers of such kind of proceedings; and we have seen how many ways they are ready to take advantage of our brethren's subscriptions since.

" To add but one thing more, we did not think it proper to subscribe, because if this humour were complied with, we could not tell where it would stop.

They conclude with these admirable words :—

" We cannot consent to what in our apprehension has such a tendency, especially in present circumstances, to narrow the Christian and Protestant liberty of the people, and to divert them from attending to *practical religion*. In some points and cases we may no doubt submit to *legal demands*, when yet we ought by no means to countenance it when there is no *pretence* of authority. But if we will bind ourselves to humane decisions in the deepest points of revelation, as if they were absolutely necessary to communion, will not the natural consequence be the lessening of people's regards to the *Word of God*, and placing undue regard to the *words of men*. Nor should men be led into *curious enquiries* about these things, in which even superior capacities lose themselves, and by which the minds of people will be taken off from the plainer truths and duties of religion And what will truth itself avail if it be not improved into Holiness ? or if it be made instrumental to destroy or abate that Charity which is the bond of perfect ness, and the fulfilling of the law ?"

Thus wrote our Presbyterian ancestors 140 years ago, still doing battle for us and for all disciples of the Lord Jesus Christ, and contending for great principles, when the conflict involved suffering and obloquy of no ordinary kind. For it was rending asunder all the ties of Christian fellowship with other Dissenters which they prized highly, and exposing them to the bitter hatred and opposition of those with whom they had so long suffered and fought, side by side, in defence of their common rights and liberties. But if the Church of Christ is to be faithful, it will doubtless, on earth, have to be a church militant to the end of its days.

After this time the change of doctrinal views in the English Presbyterian churches went on gradually and steadily through the whole of last century. " In many congregations there were at the same period those who professed Trinitarian, Arian, and Unitarian views."* It would be impossible to mark the exact times when any of them passed from one stage to another.

Where there were two ministers it often happened, as at Salter's Hall, in the Rev. Hugh Worthington's time, that one was far more heterodox than his colleague. The intercourse and connexion of these various parties in the Presbyterian Church, however, " was continued. They did not forget their common origin," nor, I may add, their great principles of freedom and desire for Catholic union, " and no offence was occasioned by disagreements respecting controversial questions. They had seen and endeavoured to avoid the evil consequences to society," and the Christian Church, as well as the little aid to truth arising out of an angry intolerant spirit of dictation. To check an evil so opposed to religious feeling, that course was adopted which tolerating the opinions of all, bound none to obedience to any, but left each man to pursue his own enquiries, and to adhere to those doctrines of which he could conscientiously approve. By promoting these ends, unanimity upon what they held to be the greater points of religion, appeared to them most likely to become general. To make Christianity comprehensive in its design, to open its benefits to all, was the distinguishing principle of their conduct; strongly contrasting with the narrow character and hopelessness of the doctrine of Election."†

These Presbyterians loved truth. They were faithful to it through good and ill report. And the Lord gave them their reward, leading them on to larger and deeper views of the Divine Word. And when we look, on the one hand, at the terrible evils caused by corruptions of that Word, whether introduced by Heathen converts, speculative schoolmen, Romish priests, or Calvinistic divines, and on the other, at the painful struggles and costly sacrifices whereby earnest men of the orthodox persuasions are slowly freeing themselves in various directions from the trammels and heavy burdens of their creed, " with a great sum obtaining their freedom," our hearts may well be filled

* History, &c., p. 28.　　　　† History, &c. p. 29.

with reverence and gratitude to those great and good men who by their faithfulness have made us to be "free born."

Towards the end of last century several devout and faithful men, seceding from the established church and the ranks of the Independents, Baptists, &c., on the ground of doctrinal objections to the popular creeds, united themselves with the English Presbyterians, and gradually introduced the name "Unitarian" among our churches. This change of title caused no change in the regular succession of worshippers in those churches, nor in their right to the institutions and property of their ancestors. Chapels, burying-grounds, endowments, assemblies, charities, and all our other institutions continued to be handed down from one generation to another to the present day, just as they had been during the whole of last century. And when our Independent brethren tried to wrest these possessions from our hold, Parliament protected us because our forefathers, in the strength of their glorious trust in the principles they had so long upheld, *had imposed no creed or theological conditions* to restrict their descendants in the search after Bible truth, or to bribe them into a rejection of the Light from whatever quarter it might come.

Several Unitarian congregations have been formed during the present century, with which the English Presbyterian societies have been associated in amicable friendship. But even in these, no subscription to any kind of creed is required, beyond what is necessarily implied in taking a doctrinal name, and trusts or funds among Unitarians are rarely fettered by doctrinal requisitions. An honourable understanding that minister and people should be in harmony as far as possible on great fundamental principles practically, of course, limits the freedom of the pulpit in both denominations. But there are no formal theological or ecclesiastical barriers to prevent English Presbyterians, at all events, from following the light of Scripture Truth wherever it may lead them, without forfeiting their name or abandoning their position.

It is no part of my present endeavours to vindicate the truth of the doctrinal results at which the English Presbyterians in general arrived by the close of the last century, in consequence of the spiritual freedom they had thus so nobly claimed, and latterly through the influence of Priestley, Lindsey, and other earnest men. It may be true that they have restored to their rightful and all-important position in Christian theology some of the grandest and most blessed of God's revealed truths. It may prove hereafter that the Christian Church of the 20th century, while lamenting various important deficiencies in what is now usually called Unitarianism, may acknowledge itself to lie under the deepest obligation for what English Presbyterians and Unitarians have done in accepting, proclaiming, and defending at the cost of so much suffering and sacrifice, certain Unitarian doctrines,—may confess that all the services the English Presbyterian section of the universal church conferred during its previous existence in resisting Romish idolatry or Protestant tyranny, were inferior to the theological work which it has since done for Christendom. But however that may be, it cannot be maintained too earnestly that nothing but good, that is a balance or *net result* of good, in the largest possible measure God is willing to grant, can result from faithfulness to the principles acted on and proclaimed by our fathers, both among the laity and ministry, throughout last century. It is quite true that their churches during the last fifty years have in many places greatly declined, and in many others become altogether extinct. But the cause of that declension may not have been *too much* devotedness to religious freedom, too faithful an opposition to anything like the imposition of a creed, to any attempt to stereotype a particular form of dogmatic belief, and fix it on the Presbyterian body as the symbol. Precisely the reverse may be found to be nearer the truth, and the decline of English Presbyterianism may be discovered to be co-temporaneous with, and *partially* caused by, indifference to English Presbyterian traditions on the part of our fathers, and a certain amount of *un*faithfulness to the memories of Salter's Hall. The Wolverhampton and Lady Hewley suits startled them into a consciousness of the singular position into which they had allowed themselves to descend from the lofty

ground which their ancestors had won and held for so
many generations. And as they found themselves about
to be stripped of the chapels, burying-grounds, and endowments bequeathed by the piety of by-gone days, they began
to ask if they had not already in some sorrowful degree
stripped *themselves* of that which was more precious still,
the principles, traditions, and name which bound them to a
glorious past, and the want of which was then the cause of
their being thus invaded and spoiled. Most of the Unitarians
of 1830 were indeed the legitimate representatives and descendants of the English Presbyterians of Elizabeth's reign,
of the Commonwealth, and of Salter's Hall. They still met,
as they do now, at the Presbyterian Board in London, in the
body of Presbyterian Ministers of London and Westminster
with the same right of addressing the throne as was granted
to their fathers on the accession of William III. They
still held their annual meetings of the Provincial Assembly
of Presbyterian Ministers of Lancashire and Cheshire
(which was founded in 1646, and has continued in unbroken
connexion to the present year), and the annual assembly of
Presbyterian Divines in the West of England (established
in 1655). They had and still have their Presbyterian College
at Carmarthen, existing in one form or other for more than a
century. The English Unitarians of the 19th century
when closely examined were clearly the lineal descendants
of the great men of a former day; and great men of the
present day, though startled at their claims, when once
convinced of the singular fact, rose one after another, night
after night, in the British senate to declare their convictions; so that at length, in spite of all the thunders of
bigotry, the rapacity of injustice, and the treachery of a sect
that had out-lived the nobleness of its youth, when Philip
Nye and Robinson, Milton, Cromwell, and Vane were its
leaders, English Unitarians were acknowledged to be the
true inheritors of English Presbyterian property and institutions. But who except their fellow-dissenters, the men
who up to 1820 or 1830 had been constantly associated
with them in various institutions, not as Unitarians, but as
English Presbyterians, and who *knew* the gradual changes
in doctrine through which their brethren had passed,—

who, of the general public, was to blame for not recognizing them in the strange masquerading habit they had donned for the season? Who among the descendants of the Heywoods and Henrys, the spiritual children of Baxter and Howe, had any right to complain when they were taken for a little controversial sect founded by Priestley and Lindsey fifty years before?

Whether it is now possible or desirable to claim and wear the great name which was once so honoured and prized, but which we have allowed to be torn from us and cast aside as useless lumber, must be discussed within wider limits than those of the present essay. But it is a matter which admits of no discussion, no compromise, and no procrastination, that we—the descendants and representatives of one of the noblest fellowships, taken for all in all, that figure in history—should not allow our precious possession of such a relationship to the past to be ignominiously lost, buried out of sight under comparatively recent and dogmatic titles; still more that we should not suffer our inheritance of the great principles of our forefathers in regard to the sufficiency of the Scriptures, freedom from creeds *even in a name*, the fullest right of private judgment and especially their cherished longing for true Christian Union, to be recklessly trampled on, or secretly betrayed. That would indeed be one of the most fatal acts of treachery to a solemn and very precious trust that the Church has ever witnessed, or the world applauded. But already there are symptoms of the re-awakening of our denomination to a clearer consciousness of its position, duties, and rights. A conviction is beginning to be widely diffused among us that English Presbyterianism (not as expressive of attachment to Presbyterian Government, but to those mighty principles above enumerated), affords a truer, wider, *and more Christian* basis for Church union than attachment to a particular Christian doctrine however important and glorious that doctrine may be. There is a growing perception (not in our own denomination only), that,—inasmuch as no sect or individual has ever attained, or can attain, to absolute truth, but that all must learn from one another, and even submit to find irreconcileable difficulties in the way of their all viewing Christian truths in the same light,—the true bond of union in the Church of Christ must be found in attachment to a Person not to a doctrine, in our common union *with* Christ, not in our common belief *about* him. It has has been said, that "the more earnestly we revive the old Presbyterian traditions, the more widely do we separate ourselves from these kindred churches," viz., the American, French, German, and Transylvanian Unitarians. But, with due deference, this could only be said in forgetfulness of what those Presbyterian traditions really are. For in their *gradual* and natural developement, they present precisely those conditions which afford the greatest facilities and attractions for union with all churches and all Christians "who love the Lord Jesus Christ in sincerity; first, in their vindication of the rights of the human soul, and defence of that liberty without which there can be neither union nor life; secondly, in their deep-rooted regard for the Holy Scriptures, as containing God's revealed word; thirdly, in their fervent aspirations for Christian Catholic union, without distinction of creeds, names, or ceremonies. They tend, indeed, "to separate us" from any church, or from that characteristic in any church, which makes either doctri nes or forms the ground of separation from other churches, but they tend irresistibly to unite us, not with "Newton, Milton," and Channing only, not with Paul and Peter, Origen and Ulphilas, Servetus, Socinus, or Coquerel alone,—but with Chrysostom, Bernard, and Augustine also, with Thomas à Kempis, Luther, Zinzendorf, Wesley, Maurice, and with all who in future ages shall blend their piety, earnestness, and faith with larger sympathies or greater light. This is the "comprehensive holy fellowship" for which we have to strive and pray, to which English Presbyterian, will conduct us far more certainly than Unitarian, traditions, even though it is true that these carry us back to the days of Arius and the apostles, and across the seas to the East and to the West. But it is not less certain, perhaps even more vitally important, to observe, that it is in the former traditions we find the surest guarantees for gradual progress in Scriptural knowledge, and the discovery of God's revealed truth—far surer than in any attempt to impose a particular set of opinions, or belief in a special doctrine, upon our churches as the settled and permanent form of Christian belief. This is a consideration of unspeakable moment to us and to our children. Our brethren of Independent churches are daily becoming more alive to it, and many of them are returning to the freer and more Christian views of religious liberty which characterised their brightest days, when the parting words of John Robinson to the pilgrim fathers, and his glorious spirit, still guided and inspired them, and when by the grace of God they put other sects to shame. If they persevere in this path, they will assuredly reap their reward in receiving yet larger supplies of Divine truth, and of the Holy Spirit. Most important of all is it to remember that the spirit of Christian love, of Christian benevolence, and loving fellowship cannot flourish in a controversial atmosphere. must breathe most freely in a church that is based upon affectionate loyalty to the loving Saviour, than in one that is formed by community of doctrinal opinion. Let us earnestly pray that we whose fathers came forth from the house of bondage to human creeds and articles a century and a half ago, may not be " again entangled" in *any* " yoke of bondage," but remembering how they may even now be looking down upon us, watching with anxious hope or fear the part we play in this eventful period of our country's history, and especially of the Christian Church, may we lay aside every weight, though it be but a name, and however endeared it may be to us, with the sins that do so easily beset us, and run with patience the race that is set before us," looking unto Jesus," not unto our frail and fallible fellow-men.

So we may hope that the river which once was known far and wide, but of late has seemed to be swallowed up in sands, uncared for and forgotten, may at length re-emerge in bright and gladdening power, bearing precious freight of Christian hearts on its consecrated tide, as it rolls onwards to the ocean of Christ's universal Church, which is finally to absorb all those streams on earth and in heaven in which the " water of life" flows freely.

APPENDIX.

The following extracts from a letter by the Rev. Dr. Mc.Crie, of Great Ormond-street, London, to the editor of the *Manchester Weekly Advertiser*, May 1, 1858, are subjoined to show the extraordinary assumptions by which some of our Scotch Presbyterian brethren are manifesting their ardour to seize the crown which has been lying, not on the pillow, but the floor, while its rightful owner slept. This gentleman was the moderator of a meeting held last year in Manchester, which he calls " The English Presbyterian Synod," and he states, among other facts, that " it is quite true that the synod to which I belong have declared—1st. That Unitarians 'deny the divinity of the Lord Jesus Christ;' 2nd. That they 'pour contempt on his atonement;' 3rd. That they 'hold the name Presbyterian, whereas Unitarian is their proper designation;' 4th. That they assume the mask 'in order to claim certain emoluments.' These, Sir, are no new charges ; they have been repeatedly preferred and proven ; and regarding ourselves as the legitimate representatives of the Presbyterians of the Commonwealth, we feel ourselves deeply aggrieved and injuriously compromised in the estimation of the English public, by being thus identified " with a party holding opinions not more at variance with our creed as Trinitarians, than with that of the venerable men whom we represent." It appears that the indignation of this synod, which is an assembly of Scotchmen living in England, had been more especially and recently excited by noticing that the *true* English Presbyterians had been presuming to exercise the right handed down to them from the accession of William III., of presenting an address to the throne, on the marriage of the young Princess, and had also petitioned Parliament in favour of a bill which they themselves opposed. This seemed to the zealous upholders of Scotch Presbyterianism in England an utterly unintelligible act of presumption, and hence these unpleasant and unhistorical remarks. But the Scotch Presbyterians are *not* the representatives or inheritors of English Presbyterianism; and even if we did commit a final act of *felo de se*, or were feloniously stifled by our northern fellow-Christians, they would have no shadow of a claim to our ancient memories or our present possessions, and for their own peace of mind, here and hereafter, had better bear with us in our folly, and not commit deeds of injustice and misrepresentation under a mistaken sense of duty, or through imperfect acquaintance with English history. Moreover we are not yet dead. Perhaps not sleeping.

Dr. M'Crie asks concerning us, "Why are they so anxious to sail under the banner of Presbyterianism, when it is notorious that they have nothing of Presbyterianism but the name?" Perhaps, if the foregoing pages should ever meet his eye, he will see that we have all of English Presbyterianism which English Presbyterians have ever had since the days of Cromwell, and that is by far the best part of it, viz, its great principles,—among which has long been a love of fair play. This is better than a name, or even than regular synodical action.

The following letters are also reprinted from the "Inquirer," as a passing commentary on the foregoing Essay, and as practical illustrations of the facts and views above stated, in some measure filling up the interstices of the historical sketch.

DEAR SIR,—I think your readers should return you thanks for your recent articles on "Unitarian Defections." . . . . Will you permit me to say, however, in the first place, that I do not think you sufficiently appreciate the value of our Presbyterian descent and traditions, nor the importance of maintaining the position which we inherit. You speak well, and with deep truth, of the necessity for widening our section of the Christian Church, of meeting the wants of various minds, of combining both the Protestant and Catholic elements therein. But are you not aware that it is our Presbyterianism from which we

receive our aspirations for this noble freedom, this catholicity of purpose and spirit ? Unitarianism in this country has been narrow and restricted. I honour English Unitarians and Unitarianism from my heart. But I should be ignorant of their history if I did not know that with the zeal of a persecuted sect contending manfully for grand and neglected truths, they naturally combined a certain bigotry and onesideness, entirely opposed to the views you advocate, and which, I am well persuaded, has had much to do with "defections" we deplore. One of our ablest and worthiest writers has truly said, "Intense exclusive conviction, fastened on a single object, and discerning truth and right in nothing else, is the frame of mind, however unworthy of the philosopher, that fits men for decided, vigorous action, and leads to immediate practical results."
—(*Retrospect of Religious Life in England, p.* 196, *2nd edition.*)

When noble-hearted men like Lindsey, Priestley, Belsham, Aspland, and a host of others, threw off the dogmatic fetters that bound them, and, purchasing their freedom "with a great price," left the Established Church and Independent body to dwell among our "free-born" Presbyterian fathers, they brought with them those "intense exclusive convictions" which enabled them to do the work they had to do. For this let us, who enter into their labours and victories, be humbly and devoutly grateful. But I believe you are looking in the wrong direction when you seek for greater catholicity of spirit and practice from the representatives of the Unitarian traditions and element in our body. You are rightly anxious to preserve the Arian form of thought as one of the elements of the Unitarian theology, and you contend earnestly for what is still more important, the necessity of "recognising the presence of our blessed Lord as inspiring and leading on the Church" at the present day. But you know that the men who inaugurated the Unitarian movement in this country strenuously resisted both these doctrines, and strove hard to confine the name of Unitarian to believers in the simple humanity of Christ. Did you ever happen to read of a meeting of a few Presbyterian ministers last century, in which the Rev. Hugh Worthington, of Salter's Hall, London, and the Rev. Benjamin Carpenter, of Stourbridge, took a leading part, held with the view of resisting the tide of Humanitarianism that was then rolling in upon the Presbyterian body, and of vindicating its Arianism in connection with cognate doctrines ? And do you remember the tone with which that meeting is referred to in the *Monthly Repository* ? Or the way in which Mr. Belsham and others generally spoke of Arian views, and the estimation in which they held both the name of Presbyterian (*vide Monthly Repository*), as compared with their own especial dogmas, and the far wider circle of Christian thought which it had included ? But some of them lived to see their error ; and had their valuable lives been longer spared, I believe they would have done something to counteract the narrow tendencies which have lost us many of those "gentle scholarly laymen" and "devout honourable women" you so well describe. I well remember the last of those honoured men above mentioned (Mr. Aspland) deeply regretting the extent to which the Presbyterian name and traditions had been slighted, and well nigh extinguished by the Unitarian element, and making an earnest appeal to one dear to me to aid in restoring their power.

For these and many other reasons, which it would be unreasonable to expect you could find space for, I believe we must not aim at what you term "building up a Unitarian Church," at "widening it," or glorifying it, or doing anything with it under the idea that it is, or ever can be, our "church of the Lord." It does not nor ever did contain the elements of a church universal. It was and is a section of that church, engaged in making a noble protest against certain errors and vindicating certain all-important truths. Its mission is by means of lectures, tracts, and societies to do this work, and to continue doing it until the little leaven has leavened the whole lump, which process is fast going on. But any attempts to convert a doctrinal movement, that in a century hence will have fulfilled its special mission, into a permanent ecclesiastical form—to exalt a doctrinal protest and appeal into the basis of a universal and spiritual church, substituting belief in certain doctrines (which have received, moreover, a one-sided form from the pressure of controversy), for faith in a universal Lord and Saviour as our bond of union, and thereby cutting ourselves off from that great Christian Church which is built upon the one foundation other than which "no man can lay"—is to engage in an enterprise that will be as surely fatal to our descendants as it has been injurious to us, and which will consummate for them the ruin which you too truly point to as gradually stealing upon ourselves.

But a far more vitally important question remains to be discussed, and must be yet awhile deferred. Has not the pressure of controversy caused views and doctrines of Christianity to be slighted or renounced which must be preached once again with living power if we are to retain those who now worship with us, and to gather in those who worship nowhere ? Is it not the neglect or denial of those doctrines that has been the chief cause of those "defections" which have *not* been the result of worldliness,—*perhaps* of that worldliness which has too often led to "defections ?" Leaving this matter for the present, I remain, yours faithfully,

————————.

July, 28, 1858.

————

DEAR SIR,—There was once a noble body of men in this country, who three hundred years ago gave up their position in the Established Church, and encountered imprisonment, confiscation of their property, exile, and even death, rather than conform to the semi-popish ordinances still inflicted on that Church by Queen Elizabeth. These men transmitted a like spirit to their descendants; and the great Presbyterian party, gaining strength and preserving zeal through years of persecution, formed the main body of that phalanx of freemen who fought and conquered for English rights in the Long Parliament and on Marston Moor. Twenty years later we find the old fire burning as brightly in the hearts of the children as it had done in the generation gone to its rest; and the memory of the two thousand martyrs of St. Bartholomew's-day, 1662, is not likely to perish at present. Sixty years rolled on, and we meet with this remarkable body of men still full of life, instinct with piety and zeal, assembling at an old hall in London, to perform a service for their country and the Church of Christ which, though unattended by danger of martyrdom from the civil power, was an act of the noblest moral courage, and such an offering to the Lord of that Church on behalf of the right and duty of free inquiry, and the sufficiency of God's Holy Scriptures unfettered by creeds and articles, as had probably never been offered before. Two hundred years were completed, in 1772, from the time when the first English Presbytery was established at Wandsworth, and still this brave, earnest, single-minded body of men was found pursuing its useful unostentatious course, influential and honoured, a power in the State, in the Christian Church, and in the unbelieving world. Another century will soon have elapsed, and where then will the English Presbyterian Church be found ? The Unitarians of England may rise up and say, "We have replaced them. Be thankful that we have turned an old effete organisation out of doors, and have given the world instead a sect full of youthful zeal, and the messenger of uncorrupted Christian truth." If English Unitarians, if Priestley and Lindsey, Belsham and Aspland, taking refuge from the narrow bigotry of other sects in the large liberty won by our Presbyterian fathers, have done this, I say it would require all the great services which they rendered to the cause of truth to cancel the condemnation which such an irreparable injury would have deserved. For assuredly it would be one of the saddest misfortunes that could befall the descendants of an ancestry like ours to be robbed of our name and inheritance, and converted into a sect sprung up in a night like Jonah's gourd, without a link to bind us to the virtues and martyrdoms of our English past, cut off from the precious memories of the noble dead, who, according to their light, were among the worthiest servants of God which England has ever known.* I remember not very long since an eloquent reference being made by Mr. Martineau at some meeting in the North, to the inestimable value of time-honoured political traditions, and a long-established political constitution. We may be sure that this is not less true in religious than in civil affairs. If the sight of a spendthrift, insensible to the hallowed memories of a long line of illustrious ancestors, spurning their mute appeal to him to live a manly life and emulate their heroic deeds, laying low the aged oaks and ancient towers of his old domain, even casting from him the very name of his fathers, which had once been honoured in the Senate, and a rallying cry in the van of freedom's battles—if this would be a sad and humiliating spectacle, what are we to think of such conduct in the case of the representatives of the Puritans of England and the inheritors of the churches of Oliver Heywood and Baxter, of Matthew Henry and John Taylor? Do not let us for a moment imagine that this is merely an affair of sentiment, requiring at the best but a little pensive poetical thought. Consequences of infinitely deeper moment, solemn as responsibility, and far-reaching as Christianity itself, are involved in this matter. Here is a fact of grand and deep significance—that a body of Christians who for a century and a half had been doing a brave and noble work in the world (though for the most part in that bigoted spirit which "intense and exclusive conviction" generally breeds) at length, taught by persecution and the spirit of God, emancipate themselves from the fetters which still bind their fellow Christians ; and though generally Trinitarian in doctrine, fearlessly

* I, of course, gladly recognise the antiquity in the Church of Christ of the leading Unitarian doctrine; and in the above remarks I do not for a moment deny the claims so eloquently urged at different times in your pages, to the antiquity of a Unitarian Church in Syria, Greece, Spain, and Poland. That is one question; but whether that Church, if it be one, is to supplant and extinguish the Church of the Presbyterians in England, is another; and the fact that, in this country, at the best, the Unitarian Church is a thing of yesterday remains incontrovertible.

refuse in the year of grace 1719 to impose any test upon their ministers and church, with devout trust commit themselves to the unrestricted pursuit of truth, and—take the consequences. We know what the *social* consequences were—obloquy, persecution, isolation. We know also the doctrinal results,—the possession, as we believe, of higher truths and purer light on several deeply important points, and on the most important of all subjects. But when, accepting our mission as their children, we endeavour to impart to others the truth and light we have ourselves received, is it not a question of the greatest practical moment whether we come before the world and the Church as the descendants and representatives of men renowned through centuries for piety, and faithfulness to conscience, for devoted love of God's holy Word; whether we appear as the advocates of Scriptural views which we have arrived at through the large-hearted trust of our ancestors in those Scriptures, and through their determination to listen to the teachings of Christ rather than the commandments of men ; or as some mushroom sect of yesterday, sprung up like the Mormons, with the general reputation, like theirs, of offering a travestie of Christianity, and of replacing the Scriptures by a Bible of our own ? Few of us but know to our sorrow how great has been the extent to which our principles have been refused a hearing, how wonderful the misunderstanding of our relation to Christ and the Scriptures even in otherwise well-informed circles, and how deadly the influence produced by reaction upon ourselves, from our having been driven from our ancestral home, and sent forth to stand upon our defence as upstart adventurers before a suspicious or hostile world. *

A great doctrinal change has been and is going forward amongst the Independents. They obtain a hearing for their views, whatever those views may be, if professedly founded on Scripture, without any greater opposition than may be offered by a growling deacon or a malignant newspaper. But we, who ought to be occupying precisely the same vantage ground, have an enormous weight of popular odium to remove, often before we can even get an hearing, still more before we can encourage those who have heard and are convinced to cast in their lot with us. Do not say that this is owing to the doctrines we preach, and would be the same under any circumstances. For who does not know how little those doctrines are understood, how constantly we find people asserting that we deny Christ,

* Truth is never more reluctantly listened to than when it is supposed to be preached for party purposes and in the interests of a sect. To give your great Unitarian truths fair play, you should be known in court as pleading for the Bible and for Christ.

astonished to discover that we use the same Bible as themselves, and exclaiming, when at length enlightened as to our faith, "Why, that is just what I have always believed?" To understand the false position into which we have got, imagine the Independents, when they find themselves agreeing to give up Calvinism, abandoning their old historic position as staunch believers in Christ and the Bible through nearly three hundred years, and stepping forth on the platform of controversy as "Grotian Christians," or "Monophysitarians," founding a "British and Foreign Homoousian Association," and throwing all their energies into the conflict with error under this new sectarian banner. Rather a suicidal policy for the descendants of men who can trace their ecclesiastical lineage up to John Robinson, Phillip Nye, Cromwell, and Milton. Yet what is their claim to stand upon Chillingworth's celebrated maxim, and to be heard as the expounders of Bible Christianity unfettered by the traditions of men, compared with that of the representatives of the men who at Salter's Hall in 1719 won the battle for a free Bible against subscription to human creeds, and who since that day in all their inherited institutions, from the Presbyterian College, Carmarthen, to Manchester College, London, have been true to their principles in the teeth of an amount of opposition and bribery that would have swept away less faithful consciences like a withered leaf in the autumn breeze?

But is there any practical solution of the difficulty, any escape from the Caudine Forks? Is the three hundredth anniversary of the founding of our denomination to come round, ere long, and find a mere ragged remnant of the once glorious Puritan and Presbyterian Church of England; with even that remnant fast vanishing into the Established Church on the one hand, or being absorbed into a controversial sect on the other? You are aware how perseveringly the Scotchmen settled in England are labouring to set their hoof upon us, hoping to tread out the last spark of life in a feeble and degenerate Church, which they regard now as composed of a few impostors and infidels. I know there are some among us who would shut their eyes both to the evil and the shame of such a termination. But I know that there are also many deeply alive both to the nobleness of their Presbyterian ancestry, and to the incalculable importance of preserving the principles and vantage-ground handed down to us by them. The members of the Provincial Assembly of Lancashire and Cheshire, who lately held their two hundredth anniversary; the Presbyterian ministers of London, who have had the right of addressing the Throne for nearly the same period; the managers of the Presbyterian Board, which has met regularly since the Revolution, and of the Presbyterian College, Carmarthen, which in one form or other has subsisted for a century and a-half; the trustees of the Manchester New College; and especially those descendants of the two thousand ejected ministers who have hitherto withstood all the temptations to desert the Church of their fathers,—cannot be insensible to the claims of that Church, nor indifferent to its fate, though, like Jerusalem, after the Captivity, its wall may be "broken down, and the gates thereof burned with fire," and the days of its prosperity seemingly ended. It will be dearer to generous hearts in its desolation than in the season of its pride and power.

I do not believe that any sudden revival is possible, or that any spasmodic efforts for such reanimation are desirable. But before all our old Nonconformist families are gone over to the State Church, and the Scotch Church in England has finally pushed us from our stools, let us not doubt that some steps might be taken to vindicate our true position and our historical antecedents. The proceedings connected with the Matthew Henry testimonial furnish an admirable and unforced opportunity. Could not a meeting of representatives of English Presbyterianism be held some time this year, to draw up and subscribe to a statement of its past history and present position, which, if circulated by thousands of copies through the country, might not only do incalculable service to the principles for which our fathers struggled, of free inquiry and the sufficiency of the Scriptures, *but also* to the cause of those doctrinal truths which their faithfulness has given us the inestimable privilege of receiving?*—a statement, moreover, which might not merely interest the educated and inquiring in our tenets, but might awaken enduring love and reverence for our fathers' faithful testimony and the history of our Church in the hearts of our children. Had that history been affectionately commended in their youth to the existing generation of our old Presbyterian families, would it not have saved many of them from deserting the cause of religious freedom for the attractions of a State-Established Church?

I said in a former letter that I had reason to know that one of the eminent men mentioned above, Mr. Aspland, deeply regretted, in his later life, having done so much to overwhelm English Presbyterianism beneath Unitarianism;

---

* In connection with this subject let me refer to Mr. Thom's valuable sermon, "Religion not Theology, the Want of the Times;" and the able article in the *National Review*, on "The Religion of the Working Classes."

and I remember well that, at the close of the conversation I then alluded to, after strongly urging the duty of endeavouring to revive the former, he added, with great animation, "If we had but had a general representative meeting, years ago, of all our Presbyterian congregations, and, after stating our history and claiming our connection with the past, had then formally re-organized ourselves under a more suitable name [he *may* have said, 'under the Unitarian name,' but I do not remember his using the word], we should not be in our present unfortunate position." One who bears Mr. Aspland's honoured name, and worthily fills his father's pulpit, has shown, in various ways, the interest he feels in the past history of English Presbyterianism. The descendants of Matthew Henry have been recently stung into a consciousness of their relation to the past by disingenuous bigotry. The proposition to appoint a missionary has roused the Provincial Assembly of Lancashire and Cheshire, to consider its origin, meaning, and responsibilities. Many signs concur to give us hope for a blessing on any manly, faithful endeavour to vindicate our position and regain our rights. Providence gave us one invaluable warning and opportunity in the danger and the deliverance commemorated by the Dissenters' Chapels Bill. If it be disregarded, we can hardly complain should we be left to perish. But was that a mere sordid struggle to keep possession of a few endowments, and of certain heaps of stone and mortar connected therewith? Or was there not an earnest desire also to maintain the cause and fulfil the purposes to which those buildings and endowments had been consecrated,—a free Bible, a progressive theology, and a Scriptural Church? Was there no sacred affection and reverence for the memories which hallowed the chapels and the tombs of our fathers? Or were the pure emotions which animated us then under the pressure of hostile injustice to fade away as worthless sentiment, without leading to effective action when the danger was past and the deliverance forgotten? *Exitus acta probat.* Let us make a pilgrimage to the ruins of Sardis and Laodicœa and consider our ways, ere it be finally too late.

Forgive my presumption, if I have said a word that is uncalled for, and believe me, yours truly,

March 16, 1859.